WHAT'S THAT NOISE?

For Claude,
Philipp, and Alexander

WHAT'S THAT NOISE?

MICHÈLE LEMIEUX

KIDS CAN PRESS LTD.
TORONTO

Printed by permission of Otto Maier Verlag

First Canadian edition published August 1989

CANADIAN CATALOGUING IN PUBLICATION DATA

Lemieux, Michèle
  What's that noise?

Translation of: Was hört der Bär?
ISBN 0-921103-69-7

I. Title.

PS8573.E546W313 1989   jC833   C89-094309-5
PZ7.L53738Wh 1989

Kids Can Press Ltd.
29 Birch Avenue
Toronto, Ontario, Canada M4V 1E2

With kind appreciation to Morrow Junior Books, William Morrow and Company, Inc., New York, for their help in the production of the Canadian edition.

Printed and bound in Hong Kong by Wing King Tong Company Limited

89 0 9 8 7 6 5

WHAT'S THAT NOISE?

 big brown bear woke from a deep sleep.
I heard a noise, he thought, a funny little noise.
And I can still hear it. It's not the noise that mice make.
My noise is not a *squeak-squeak* noise.

Brown Bear stretched and yawned.
Have I slept through the whole winter,
he wondered, or for only one night?
Suddenly he felt very hungry.

But the funny little noise was not his stomach growling.
It was not the baby birds in their nest. *Peep. Peep.*
It was not the frogs by the stream. *Ribit. Ribit.*

Brown Bear came to the edge of the woods. "I am looking for my noise," he told the tree. "It is not a squeak-squeak noise. It is not a peep-peep noise. It is not a ribit-ribit noise."

"Is it the woodcutters?" said the tree.
"Their axes go *chock, chock.*"
But Brown Bear said, "No, that is not my noise.
My noise is not a chock-chock noise."

Brown Bear stopped to see if the fish knew what the noise was. "It is not a squeak-squeak, peep-peep, ribit-ribit, or chock-chock noise," said the bear.

"Well," said the fish, "is it the water wheel of the old mill, turning in the stream? It goes *creak-splash, creak-splash*."

"No," said Brown Bear. "That is not my noise. My noise is not a creak-splash noise."

Brown Bear climbed high on a cliff. An owl lived
up there. "Can you hear my noise?" said Brown Bear.
"It is not a squeak-squeak, peep-peep,
ribit-ribit, chock-chock, or creak-splash noise."

But the owl said, "I don't know about your noise. I only know when it's time for my dinner. And that is right now."

Brown Bear remembered that he was hungry, too.

He walked on until he saw a farm. The farmer
and his wife were going to pick vegetables.

"My, those tomatoes look juicy good," said the
bear. Then he thought, I will make a big noise.
He tossed an apple into the duck pond. *Splash!*
The ducks and geese squawked, the farmer and
his wife turned around . . .

. . . and Brown Bear snatched a whole basket of tomatoes
while no one was looking.

He hid behind a bush and ate them up while
the watchdog got a scolding.

But then the noise came back—*thump-bump,*
thump-bump. If I eat some honey, thought Brown Bear,
it may go away. And if it doesn't, the honey will still
taste sweet. Soon it will be dark. Then I will creep
up to the beehives on soft, soft paws—

"Ouch!" The bees stung Brown Bear on the nose,
where it hurt. He ran away as fast as he could. And
as he ran he heard that noise again—*thump-bump,*
thump-bump.

The night was turning cold, dark, and wet.
"*Brrr,*" said Brown Bear. "My fur is freezing.
I want to go back to my den."

But—*thump-bump, thump-bump.* Brown Bear
thought he heard something running behind him.
He ran even faster.

Home at last, Brown Bear watched the sun
come up. The noise was quieter now, and slower,
as if it was tired from running, too.

Brown Bear began to feel sleepy.
It was time for the birds to fly south.
And it was time for his long winter nap.

Just then Brown Bear found the
noise. It is inside me, he thought.
It is my heart beating. That is what
it was all the time.

Brown Bear is sleeping very deeply now.
But one morning, when the snow has melted,
he will wake from his long sleep and hear
his heart beating once again, and then he
will know . . .

. . . that it is spring.

And the big brown bear will dance for joy.

Michèle Lemieux was born in Quebec and has worked as an illustrator of books and magazines. Her work has been published internationally in France, Germany, the United Kingdom, the United States, Canada and Japan. She is the illustrator of the highly acclaimed picture-book version of *Amahl and the Night Visitors* by Gian Carlo Menotti, as well as Eveline Hasler's *Winter Magic* and *A Gift from Saint Francis* by Joanna Cole. She lives in Montreal with her husband.